THE POTTAMUS FAMILY
AND
THE UNHAPPY POTTAMUS

Written and Illustrated by
Amy E. Scheiding
Angela M. Sundberg
Marcia L. Scheiding

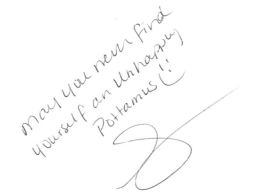

May you never find
yourself an Unhappy
Pottamus!

DORRANCE PUBLISHING CO., INC.
PITTSBURGH, PENNSYLVANIA 15222

Dedicated to

Kaylee Jade
and
Alexander William

Wishing you many happy days.

ISBN-10: 0-8059-7478-4
ISBN-13: 978-0-8059-7478-2

Printed in the United States of America

First Printing

For more information or to order additional books, please contact:
Dorrance Publishing Co., Inc.
701 Smithfield Street
Third Floor
Pittsburgh, Pennsylvania 15222-3906
U.S.A.
1-800-788-7654
www.dorrancebookstore.com

It was a beautiful
day at Pottamus Pond.
The sun was shining and
the birds were singing.

Papa Pottamus was busy gathering moss and reeds from Pottamus Pond.

Mama Pottamus was making
lunch for the Pottamus family.

Baby Pottamus was playing on the floor with his Pottamus toys.

All of a sudden, Mama Pottamus
heard Baby Pottamus crying.

Baby Pottamus is too young to talk. When Baby Pottamus needs something, he cries and becomes an Unhappy Pottamus.

Mama Pottamus knew Baby Pottamus
became an Unhappy Pottamus when he was hungry.

Mama Pottamus said, "You will feel better after lunch my little Unhappy Pottamus".

Mama Pottamus called to Papa Pottamus. "It is time to eat. We have a very Unhappy Pottamus."

Mama, Papa and Baby Pottamus sat down to eat. Although lunch
was very good, Baby Pottamus was still an Unhappy Pottamus.

Mama Pottamus said, "Baby Pottamus probably needs his diaper changed."

Papa agreed and said, "Yes, a wet diaper always makes Baby Pottamus an Unhappy Pottamus." Papa changed his diaper, but Baby Pottamus was still an Unhappy Pottamus.

Papa Pottamus said, "Maybe Baby Pottamus has a booboo. A booboo always turns Baby Pottamus into an Unhappy Pottamus."

Papa and Mama looked at Baby Pottamus' knees, they looked at his toes, and they even looked at his nose. They could not find a booboo anywhere. Baby was still an Unhappy Pottamus.

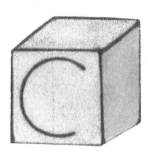

Mama Pottamus said, "Maybe Baby Pottamus was getting a new tooth. That always makes him an Unhappy Pottamus."

Mama looked to see if Baby Pottamus was getting a new tooth, but he was not getting any new teeth.

Baby Pottamus was still an Unhappy Pottamus.

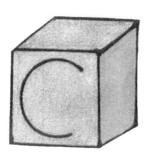

Papa Pottamus told Mama Pottamus, "Baby Pottamus likes to swim. If he doesn't get to swim, he becomes a very Unhappy Pottamus."

Papa Pottamus took Baby Pottamus to swim in the pond. Baby Pottamus swam for a little while, then he began to cry and turned into an Unhappy Pottamus.

Papa Pottamus was taking Baby Pottamus back to the house. On the way, Baby Pottamus stopped crying.

Papa smiled when he looked back to see his little Unhappy Pottamus was sound asleep.

When Papa and Baby Pottamus got home, Mama Pottamus whispered, "Oh, of course, he always turns into an Unhappy Pottamus when he is tired."

Mama Pottamus put Baby Pottamus into his bed for a nap.

When Baby Pottamus woke up, he was a very Happy Pottamus.

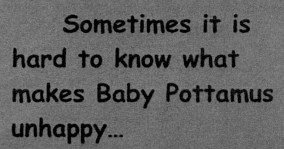

Sometimes it is hard to know what makes Baby Pottamus unhappy...

But Mama and Papa know they can make Baby Pottamus happy again.